The Midnight Ghosts

Emma Fischel

Illustrated by Adrienne Kern

Adapted by Jane Bingham

Reading Consultant: Alison Kelly
Roehampton University

Contents

Chapter 1

An invitation

Adam and Sally Midnight read their letter excitedly. "It's from Aunt Crystal!" said Sally. "We haven't seen her for years."

"Why's she writing to us?" Adam asked, reading over Sally's shoulder.

Twelve Bells End
Gloomwood Road
Middle-Knight-on-Sea

December 4

Dear Sally and Adam,

I hope you are well. Would you like to come
and stay? Uncle Matt and I have to go away
next week and it would be lovely for your cousin
Max to see you after so many years.

Hope you can come!

Love and kisses,
Aunt Crystal
xxx

"Great!" said Adam. "They live in a big old house. We can explore."

Sally didn't reply. She was looking at the photo Aunt Crystal had sent with her letter.

Matt, me and darling Max

"So that's Max," Adam said. "I hope he likes cats." Adam didn't go anywhere without his cat, Tigs.

"I hope he likes us," said Sally.

Chapter 2

Lost in the dark

Early the next Monday, Sally and Adam and Tigs raced for the train to Middle-Knight-on-Sea.

6

It was a long journey but, at first, they were busy thinking about what they would do.

The train sped past smoky towns and bustling cities. Sally listened to her music. Adam found the buffet car.

The train rattled on, past
villages and into a dark forest.
Sally listened to her music again.

Adam made
another trip to
the buffet car.

Purrr...

Zzzzzzzzzzzzz...

Hours later,
the train
trundled
over a bleak
moor.

At last, they arrived at the final stop, Middle-Knight-on-Sea. Adam and Sally stumbled out onto the platform and looked around. It was completely deserted.

They waited and waited, but no one came. As they were beginning to despair, a ghostly figure loomed out of the shadows.

I think it wants us to follow...

Before Sally could stop him, Adam had run after the figure. It led them away from the station, down a gloomy, overgrown path. An owl hooted and Sally jumped.

Then, without warning, the figure disappeared.

I know where we are!

"What now?" Sally asked. "We're totally lost." But Adam had spotted a road sign.

A minute later, they were staring up at Twelve Bells End.

Chapter 3

Journey's end

Sally knocked boldly on the front door. There was the sound of approaching footsteps, the door slowly opened and a grim-faced woman peered at them.

Yeeess?

Adam and Sally took one look at the spooky maid and were about to run, when a second person appeared.

"Hello," said Max.

"I thought it must be you."

Do come in.

Taking a deep breath, Adam and Sally followed Max inside.

He led his cousins into a dimly-lit hallway, full of family paintings and statues.

That's Great Aunt Mildred, next to the urn.

Then he marched them up a creaking staircase...

through a maze of passageways...

...until they reached Adam and Sally's room.

"Make yourselves at home," said Max. "Dinner is at seven. It's fried newt wrapped in tongue – yum!" He strolled off down the corridor, licking his lips.

Brrrrrr. It's cold up here.

"This place gives me the creeps!" whispered Adam.

"Me too," said Sally. "And I don't like the sound of dinner, either."

As they looked around their eerie room, lightning streaked across the window. A gust of icy air made them shiver and somewhere a clock started chiming loudly.

"Look over there!" cried Sally, pointing at an old desk.

Pages were tearing off a calendar and days of the month were spinning to the floor. A ghostly shadow flitted across the wall.

"HELP!" Adam and Sally yelled together, running to the door.

Chapter 4

Dinner is served

Please welcome our guests, Adam and Sally.

Sally and Adam were still trembling when they arrived downstairs for dinner. But the meal did nothing to calm their fears.

Everyone around the table looked extremely odd and their conversation made no sense.

As for the food, it was absolutely disgusting.

You'll love the Slug Surprise.

Adam and Sally ate as little as possible. Even a haunted room was better than mustard ice cream.

Yum!

Tigs, on the other hand, was in cat heaven.

Chapter 5

Restless night

Adam and Sally climbed quickly into bed.

"I'm sure we'll feel better in the morning," said Sally, bravely.

ZZZZZZZ...

They hadn't been asleep long when a heavy thump woke them. A large notebook had landed on the floor. As they watched, wobbly lines began to appear on its pages...

Yeowww!

HELP!

A second later, the wardrobe door creaked open.

An invisible hand was writing on the dusty mirror.

Sally and Adam clung to each other as an icy wind whooshed into the room. It lifted up a tattered newspaper from the fireplace and carried it over to Sally.

Horror at Twelve

At twelve o'clock last night, Mervin Midnight (52) was hit on the head by a jar of pickled lizards.

Twelve Bells End

The accident happened at Twelve Bells End, the Midnight family home.

Indeed, every year, as the clock strikes midnight on December 12, strange accidents have happened at the Midnights' mansion.

Mervin Midnight is recovering well. He has decided to give up his job at the bank and join the circus instead.

Latest victim: Mervin Midnight

"Mervin Midnight was one of the strange men at dinner!" cried Sally.

Bells End

Other Midnight victims

The strange accidents have had lasting effects on the unfortunate Midnight victims.

Famous dancer, Posy Midnight, fell down a flight of stairs. She has recently been spotted playing soccer.

Posy Midnight on stage

Joker Midnight slipped on a banana skin. Friends say he now prefers mathematics to jokes.

Joker playing tricks

Mildred Midnight and Arthur Midnight suffered even worse accidents. Unfortunately, neither of them survived.

SUNDAY SCORCHER December 13

"This house isn't safe," whimpered Adam.

Chapter 6

Village of fear

After a sleepless night, Adam and
Sally were up early.

"I'm starving!" said Adam.

"Let's find some decent breakfast
in the village," suggested Sally.

I couldn't
face another
meal here!

As they entered the village, everyone looked at them strangely. Some people even started whispering.

Feeling very unwelcome, Sally and Adam crept into the supermarket.

"Aren't you the visitors at Twelve Bells End?" asked the manager.

"You should leave that place immediately," hissed an old man, "before it's too late..."

Adam and Sally left the store in a hurry.

"I can't bear it here any longer," said Adam. "Can we go home?"

But before Sally could answer, a ghostly voice came from behind a wall.

Youuu whoooo!

"Go to the cottage with the red windows," it whispered. "There's someone there you need to see."

It didn't take long to find the cottage. As Sally and Adam walked up the path, they spotted a grumpy old man in the garden.

"What are you doing here?" he growled, waving his stick at them.

"We were told to come here," said Sally, confused. "We're staying at Twelve Bells End."

"What?" the old man cried, suddenly alarmed. "You must leave that house while you still can!"

"But we promised Aunt Crystal we'd stay all week," sighed Adam.

"Oh, you're related to the Midnights..." said the man, thoughtfully. "In that case, you'd better come inside."

Where shall I start?

Chapter 7

Lord Midnight's curse

Once Adam and Sally had settled down, the old man began.

I've seen dreadful things at Twelve Bells End.

"I'm Frank Forthright," he said, "and I used to be the Midnights' gardener."

"For the last fifteen years, the family has been under a dreadful curse. Every year, on the twelfth day of the twelfth month, another victim is struck down."

DONG!

"It always happens on the twelfth stroke of midnight. Some victims are killed instantly and their ghosts haunt the house. Others survive, but they are never the same again."

"There's Posy, who used to be a dancer. She had a bad fall and turned soccer crazy."

73 x 64 = 4,672!

"Young Joker slipped on a banana skin and started finding mathematics more funny than jokes."

"Then, two years ago, Mervin the banker was hit on the head. Now he wants to join the circus."

"And, of course, there's your cousin Max. After his accident last year, he only wants to eat really disgusting food."

"So all those people at dinner are victims of the Midnight curse..." said Sally.

"And the ghosts that haunt our room are victims too," added Adam with a shiver. "But why are the Midnights cursed?"

"Look here," said Frank, reaching for a book.

He thumbed through the pages, to a picture of a silver urn. "See the dark blue stone set in the urn," he said. "That's the Midnight Stone and it's the cause of all the trouble."

Adam and Sally studied the page.

The Curse of the Midnight Stone

The Midnight Stone has always been a Midnight family treasure. Set in an antique silver urn, the stone can never leave Twelve Bells End. If someone removes it from the urn, a curse will fall on the whole Midnight family. The curse can only be broken if a member of the family returns the stone to its proper place.

"I've seen that old urn by the staircase," said Adam. "But who removed the stone?"

Frank gave a sigh. "Archibald Midnight. He was a wicked man."

36

"Fifteen years ago, the family banished him and his daughter, Marcia. Before leaving the house, he wanted revenge. He quickly took the stone from the urn and hid it."

I curse you all!

"He died without telling anyone the stone's hiding place."

"Then we must search the house until we find it!" said Adam, grabbing Sally by the arm. "Come on! We're members of the family. We have to break this horrible curse."

Chapter 8

A secret room

"I'd forgotten how big the house is," said Adam gloomily, when they arrived back, ready to start searching.

"Wait a minute," cried Sally. "There's a blocked-out window next to our room. Perhaps there's another room up there."

They sprinted up the stairs and searched along the corridor.

There must be a door here somewhere...

A muffled cough made Adam pause. He turned around and saw a black figure scurrying away.

Sally was busy examining
an old oak cabinet.
"Help me shift
this," she called
to Adam.

Ow...
that's my foot!

Eventually, they
moved the heavy
cabinet away
from the wall.
There, behind
it, was a
secret door.

With trembling hands, Sally turned the door knob. Very slowly, the stiff door groaned open.

"Wow!" exclaimed Adam.

It was like stepping into a weird museum. The room was crammed full of amazing objects. Adam and Sally were about to explore when they felt an icy wind. The Midnight ghosts had arrived...

41

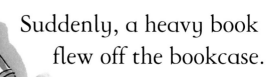

Suddenly, a heavy book flew off the bookcase.

CLUNK!

Then an ancient radio crackled into life.

Read fast before it's too late.

Adam and Sally grabbed the book and raced out of the room... straight into Max.

Hi! I've got great plans for today.

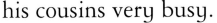

For the rest of the day, Max kept his cousins very busy.

We must get away.

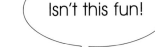

Isn't this fun!

We have to read the book.

Fa la la. Faldi-ladi-da.

After sitting through dinner – and Max's singing – Adam and Sally finally managed to escape.

43

Chapter 9

Collecting clues

They rushed to their room and picked up the book. It fell open at the last page of writing. "Lord Midnight's diary," said Sally, in excitement.

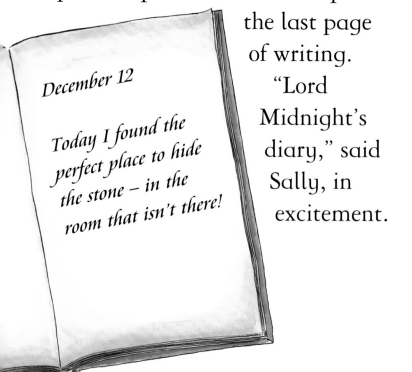

December 12

Today I found the perfect place to hide the stone – in the room that isn't there!

Adam noticed the date. "That's the day the midnight accidents happen," he said, quietly.

Sally gasped. "It's also today!"

Adam looked at his watch. "In less than two hours it will be midnight," he said. "The curse may strike *us* next..."

Not if we find the stone first...

"It says in the diary that the stone is hidden in a room that isn't there..."

That doesn't make sense!

Maybe he means the secret room.

Their hearts beating fast, Sally and Adam raced back to the secret room. There was so much stuff, the stone could be anywhere.

With a sudden icy gust, two candles lit up an oil painting. Sally looked at the painting, then looked again. A man with a funny hat on was moving his arm.

"He's pointing at something," she realized.
"Only the picture frame," said Adam.

"Then let's look there," said Sally. With trembling hands, she lifted down the painting...

pulled the canvas away from the frame...

...and spotted a folded-up piece of paper. Adam unfolded it and read a scribbled clue.

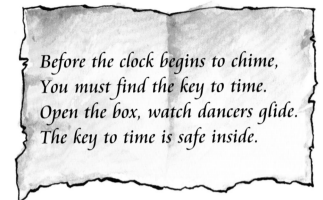

Before the clock begins to chime,
You must find the key to time.
Open the box, watch dancers glide.
The key to time is safe inside.

"What key?" puzzled Adam.

"What box?" asked Sally.

Time crept on as they searched
the cluttered room.

They were about to give up, when Adam spotted a brown box on the chest. He opened it carefully.

Inside, a set of tiny figures danced to a tinkling tune.

"Look!" he cried. "One of the musicians is playing a key."

He took the key and frowned. "The key to time... How do you unlock time?"

"Clocks tell the time," said Sally. "Maybe it's the key to a clock."

Sure enough, one turn of the key opened the big grandfather clock...

...and revealed another clue.

Look for the dancer who never leaves his place. He hides a secret behind his smiling face.

"I'm tired of riddles," said Adam with a sigh.

But Sally didn't hear. She was hurriedly scanning the room for a smiling dancer.

Adam stretched out his arms to yawn... and sent a china statue spinning to the floor!

"You clumsy oaf," said Sally, looking at the pieces of china on the carpet. Then something else caught her eye. A dark blue bag was poking out of the china fragments.

She quickly snatched it up and looked inside. At last, they'd found it – the Midnight Stone!

Chapter 10

The Midnight Stone

For a moment, Adam and Sally just stared at the stone.

"It's beautiful," sighed Sally.

"It's almost midnight," realized Adam, in a panic.

Clutching the stone, they ran to the staircase.

"Only two minutes left!" cried Sally. She stood on tiptoe and reached up to the urn. It was no good – she was far too short.

As they searched for something to stand on, Mervin Midnight appeared on the stairs.

We need help!

"Do you want an acrobat?" he asked. "I'm training to be one."

"Can you put this stone in the urn for us?" asked Adam.

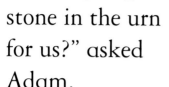

"Easy!" said Mervin, taking the stone. "I'll toss it up like a juggling ball. I'm very good at juggling." He threw the stone into the air... and nearly dropped it.

"It's not a game!" said Sally, urgently. "Please hurry."

Just then, the first
strike of midnight
sounded.

DONG!

Instantly,
a flash of lightning
lit up the sky.

DONG!

What's
happening?

The second strike
shattered a
mirror on
the wall.

DONG!

went the third strike and a whirling wind swept through the corridor.

Sally was horrified. "We're too late! The curse will claim another victim."

DONG!

On the ninth stroke, a dark shadow appeared and came closer. Sally and Adam clung to each other.

DONG!

It was the creepy maid. She walked straight up to Mervin, grabbed the stone from his hand... and placed it in the urn.

DONG!

Just in time!

On the twelfth DONG, ghostly howls filled the hall, growing fainter and fainter until they faded into nothing.

"You've broken the Midnight curse!" said Sally.

"And set the ghosts free," added Adam, staring at the strange maid.

"Only with your help," the maid replied, smiling for the first time.

But who *are* you?

"I'm Marcia," she announced, "Archibald Midnight's daughter. I wanted to break my father's curse, so I came back disguised as a maid. Now you've found the stone, perhaps the family will let me come home."

So that's why you were lurking by the secret room!

At that moment, they were joined by the other Midnights, who were no longer under the curse.

"What happened?" asked
Mervin. "Who broke the curse?"

"I did," said Marcia, "with Sally
and Adam's help."

"Is that you, Marcia?" asked Mervin. "Welcome home!"

After all the excitement, Adam and Sally were starving.

"How about a midnight feast?" suggested Max. "There's some scrumptious food in the kitchen." And this time he meant it.

Yes please!

Edited by Katie Daynes
Series editor: Lesley Sims
Cover design: Russell Punter

This edition first published in 2006 by Usborne Publishing Ltd.,
Usborne House, 83-85 Saffron Hill, London EC1N 8RT, England.
www.usborne.com
Copyright © 2006, 2004 Usborne Publishing Ltd.